UP NORTH

UP NORTH

Jeff Ross

orca soundings

ORCA BOOK PUBLISHERS

Library and Archives Canada Cataloguing in Publication

Ross, Jeff, 1973-, author
Up North / Jeff Ross.
(Orca soundings)

Issued in print and electronic formats.
ISBN 978-1-4598-1456-1 (softcover).—ISBN 978-1-4598-1457-8 (pdf).—
ISBN 978-1-4598-1458-5 (epub)

I. Title. II. Series: Orca soundings
PS8635.O6928U66 2017 jC813'.6 C2017-900821-8
C2017-900822-6

First published in the United States, 2017
Library of Congress Control Number: 2017932495

Summary: In this high-interest novel for teen readers, Rob is involved in a violent incident in a northern community.

Orca Book Publishers is dedicated to preserving the environment and has printed this book on Forest Stewardship Council® certified paper.

Orca Book Publishers gratefully acknowledges the support for its publishing programs provided by the following agencies: the Government of Canada through the Canada Book Fund and the Canada Council for the Arts, and the Province of British Columbia through the BC Arts Council and the Book Publishing Tax Credit.

Edited by Tanya Trafford
Cover image by Shutterstock.com

ORCA BOOK PUBLISHERS
www.orcabook.com

Printed and bound in Canada.

20 19 18 17 • 4 3 2 1

For Heather, who understands what it's like to live up north. And with deepest love for my wife, Megan.

Chapter One

I don't think I'll ever understand why that boy had to die. But I've spent enough time trying to figure it out, and I'm tired of it. I don't think saying that is disrespectful. It's just a fact. I'm tired, so I'm writing it all down and then I'm going to put it somewhere, and maybe years from now I'll read it and it'll make sense. I'll be able to go through these pages and understand everything like it was written on a crystal-clear northern night sky.

Though I doubt it.

I can't help but wonder how different things could have been if Chantale Hart's party hadn't sucked. I feel like there was a moment when everything might have shifted slightly, and then I wouldn't even be writing this. The road not taken. Chantale just doesn't know how to throw a party.

"That sucked," Keith said. He was our driver, behind the wheel of his mother's van, cigarette between his lips, a glassy look to his eyes.

"Washit," Joel replied. Joel had "primed" before going to the party and, once there, had inhaled a six-pack. He was no longer useful as a human being.

The van smelled like stale farts and lacrosse gear.

And something else.

"Why does she even bother?" Alan asked.

Alan was the reason I was in the stinking van. We'd met at guitar lessons. I decided to learn to play guitar after all the garbage happened back home that ended up sending my brother, Adam, to jail and a girl to her grave. I didn't blame my time DJing for what happened to Mary Jane and my brother, but I just couldn't listen to that music anymore. I even sold all my records before we moved up here. "Up North," as they say.

I'd bought a second-hand guitar and started playing Americana stuff. Josh Ritter, Ryan Adams, Bright Eyes. If any of my old DJ friends saw me now, they wouldn't recognize me at all.

Which, maybe, was the point.

Mom and I had moved here when my brother got transferred to a different youth penitentiary. I felt lucky to have met Alan on one of the first days at school, and luckier still that Alan was a good guy. The kind of guy who would seek out the new kid and try to make him feel at home.

Alan and Keith had been friends since they were little kids, which was why the two of them were together that night. Otherwise I doubt they would ever have met. Alan was kind and quiet and always a little lost-looking. Keith was what you might call the school bully. That kid who's always punching down, beating on anyone weaker than him. No doubt I would have had my head jammed under his arm on a regular basis had I not been Alan's friend. Instead I was in a van with him, cruising the wintry streets trying to find something to do after Chantale failed so horribly at throwing a party.

"Now what are we going to do?" Alan asked. He was behind me in the middle row. Joel was laid out on the back row, making horrible guttural sounds. Somehow I had managed to snag shotgun.

"No puking in the van," Keith yelled, looking in the rearview.

"Home," Joel said. Keith shook his head.

"Hey, Keith?" Alan said.

"Yeah?"

"Why do you have a bunch of rotten fruit back here?"

"Christ, *that's* the stink. That was from the lacrosse tournament. My mom was making sandwiches and shit for us. You'd think it'd be all frozen in these temperatures."

"Some of it is. The rest is squishy," Alan said. We were at a stop light, one of only three in town. The buildings outside looked as though someone had painted them entirely white.

"Take me home, country *roadssss*," Joel wailed.

"Yeah, yeah," Keith said. "By the way, *you* were supposed to be the DD, idiot."

"So sorry, sir. It won't happen again, sir."

I looked over at Keith. Something changed in his eyes as the light flicked to green. I didn't know him that well. In fact, I only hung out with him when I didn't have any other options. But at that moment he looked like a cartoon character who'd just had an idea. I was surprised there wasn't a lightbulb flashing above his head.

"I know what we can do," he said.

I didn't dare ask what. We drove in silence to the end of Joel's long lane and stopped.

"You're home," Keith said.

"Drive me in," Joel said.

Joel lived on a farm. I didn't know what happened there in the winter. Maybe they had cows or something. But anytime we'd ever picked him up, his parents and sister all seemed to be asleep. Even if it was only eight or nine o'clock.

"You sure you want that, Joeley?"

"C'mon, don't make me walk."

Keith turned into the lane. "Okay, remember you asked for it."

As we neared the house, Keith shut the headlights off.

"Don't make noise, okay?" Joel said, trying to pull himself into a seated position in the back.

"Okay, partner," Keith said. Joel's parents were very much against drinking. Joel, on the other hand, seemed to be making a career of it. He sometimes stank of whiskey after lunch at school, and I often found him at the back of the school, spitting gooey wads of chewing tobacco onto the ground rather than attending classes.

When we came to a stop, Joel made his way to the middle row and Alan opened the door.

"Thanks, man," Joel said. He kind of fell out of the van, only righting himself as he hit the slippery ground. "Don't slam the door."

"For sure," Keith whispered.

Joel gave us a little wave as he swayed and swerved to the porch. Then, just as he was about to open the door, Keith revved the engine, laid on the horn and flashed his high beams.

"Dude," Alan said.

Keith was laughing so hard there were tears in his eyes. The second-floor lights in the house all came on at once. Keith dropped the van into Reverse and spun out on the driveway. I glanced in the side-view mirror as we drove down the lane. Joel seemed to be looking for options.

Someplace to go other than inside. Then the door opened and his father's shape blocked the light from inside.

"He is going to be in so much shit," Keith said, still laughing.

"That was a dick move," Alan said.

"Yeah yeah. Maybe next time he'll actually live up to being DD. This is the third time he's pulled that trick."

So that was all it took to get Keith angry and vengeful. Not living up to your weak promise of being the designated driver. I should have known worse was to come. I should have known getting into that van was a mistake. I should have known that some people just haul hate and pettiness around with them for no good reason. Or maybe for one good reason—because it's all they've ever known.

When we hit the road, Keith turned right.

"Where we going?" Alan asked.

"To the rez," Keith said.

"Why?"

That look flashed in Keith's eyes again. "To fuck with the injuns."

Chapter Two

I'd never been to the reserve before. I knew it was there, just outside the town limits. We'd driven past it a couple of times on our way out to the youth penitentiary but hadn't ever had a reason to go in. I didn't have any friends living down those narrow streets. The native kids seemed to stick together, just like every other group at school did.

The few kids in band always huddled in a corner. The lacrosse guys bumped each other in the hallways and laughed at their own stupid jokes. And the kids from the reserve kept to themselves, in class, during lunch and in the parking lot.

"What are we doing?" Alan asked.

Keith had lit a smoke. He smoked cigarettes like they were providing him with pure oxygen. He'd light one up and take three or four really quick inhales on it before exhaling. The cigarette would burn away between his fingers until he remembered it was there, and then he'd do the same thing again. When the cigarette was a little more than half done, he'd flick it away as though it had attacked him.

The van filled with smoke. Finally he rolled the window down.

"Get that rotten fruit ready," he said.

"What for?"

"A little Thanksgiving treat," Keith said, laughing. "We'll give Tonto something to feast upon."

"What are you talking about?" Alan asked.

Keith slowed at a green light as it turned to yellow. He signaled left to go into the reserve.

"They all hang out at the stupid community-center thing they have here. It's not much bigger than a double-wide trailer, but they have dances in there every Friday night so all the kids can carry on their grand tradition of incest."

"Dude," I said. Somehow it had taken me that long to find my voice.

"What? There are, like, eight families in there. Everyone's related, and then their kids all hook up."

"That isn't even close to true," Alan said.

"Maybe not entirely, but close. Anyway, doesn't matter. Do you know Devon Warchild or whatever the fuck his last name is?"

"Devon Warren?" I said.

"Warchild, Warren, whatever. He'll be here." The light turned green, and Keith drove into the reserve.

"So what?"

"So he was hitting on Michelle last week." Keith hauled on his cigarette, then flicked it out the open window.

"I seriously doubt that," Alan said. Michelle was Keith's ex-girlfriend. They'd broken up months before, but Keith still thought they would get back together. In the meantime, he scared off every guy that came near her while graphically regaling us with every second of his and Michelle's sexual history.

"He was, man. She even came and told me about it. Said she was scared of him."

"So what? She's not your girlfriend anymore," Alan said.

Keith froze for a moment, then lit another cigarette. "Give me some of that fruit," he said.

The houses were all over the map in terms of size and shape. Everything from tiny shacks with dim lights glowing behind thin curtains to giant three-story places with second-level porches and heavy SUVs parked in the driveways.

Keith said, "You can tell who the drinkers are, right?"

To be honest, to me it looked like every other neighborhood up here.

"How can you tell?" Alan said. He'd placed the box on the console between Keith and me.

"The size of the house. The value of their precious pickup trucks. Everyone on the rez gets the same amount of money every month. It's how they do things.

Doesn't matter if you work or not. They're communists. They bring in all the cash they can, most of it from the government and then everyone gets a share. Some of them buy big houses and expensive cars, and others drink shit-tons of alcohol. Look at this place." He pointed at a building with a stack of empty Labatt 50 cases piled up against the wall.

"That looks like it could be a bar or a restaurant," Alan said.

"Bullshit. That's some drunken injun's place."

Brighter lights shone ahead of us. Keith reached into the box of rotten fruit.

"Is there another way out of here?" Alan asked.

I turned to look at him. Each street-light we passed under lit up his worried face. I could tell he didn't want to be here any more than I did.

"The road wraps around, then goes back west. We can do this and then hook up with the highway in three minutes. They won't have a second to think."

"Do what?" I said, but Keith ignored me.

"You sure?" asked Alan.

"Yeah, my dad used to bring me in here when he wanted to buy cheap gas and illegal smokes."

There was a cluster of people standing out in front of the community center, a cloud of smoke and breath around them. Keith rotated the tomato in his hand.

"This'll be perfect. It's hard enough to throw, but it will bust up when it hits him."

"How do you know he'll be out here?" Alan asked.

"If he isn't, it'll send a message." There were maybe fifteen guys standing there. A couple of them had jackets on, but most were in T-shirts or thin sweaters. "Come on, grab something."

"Nah," Alan said.

"I'd just hit you if I threw anything from over here," I said.

"Lob it over the roof," Keith said. I didn't reply, because I had no interest in throwing rotten fruit at anyone. We were moving at a crawl. As we neared, a few heads turned toward the van. "Fine—be chickenshits." Keith propped his knee on the underside of the steering wheel. Once the crowd was within earshot, he began banging on his mouth with an open palm, going, "Aye, aye, aye, aye."

The group of guys, all of whom I'd seen at school at some time or other, stared at the van.

"Happy Thanksgiving, you redskin sons of bitches!" Keith yelled. Then he hurled the tomato at the group. It hit one guy dead on and exploded over the three or four people closest to him.

Keith went back to his exaggerated noises as he stomped on the gas. "Hi-de-ho, Tonto!"

He had tears in his eyes again from laughing so hard.

"Holy shit, Keith, you got him right in the face," Alan said. I couldn't tell whether he was impressed or appalled.

"Yeah, that was a sweet shot."

"Was that Devon?" I asked.

"Maybe," Keith said. "Haven't you noticed they all look alike?"

We tore through the reserve, fishtailing down the road. We hadn't gone very far when the interior of the van got lit up by the headlights of a vehicle coming up behind us. Fast.

"Shit, man, they're after us!" Alan said.

Keith looked in the rearview mirror, then stepped on the gas. The van drifted on the slick road before catching dry pavement and shooting forward.

"Don't worry, man, we'll be out of here in no time. We can lose them behind the arena. I know a shortcut there that doubles back to the highway."

I checked the side-view mirror. There were two trucks behind us. They were taking up both sides of the road. We hit the next corner fast, Keith leaning into the turn.

"I think they're going to ram us!" Alan said.

"They aren't going to ram us. We're going to drive out of here." The road cut quickly to the right and then very suddenly came to a T.

"Which way?" I said.

"Left," Keith replied, slowing but not stopping at the intersection. "Calm down, ladies. I've got this."

"Are you sure?" Alan asked. The trucks were right behind us, one of them inches from the rear bumper. We came to another stop sign, and Keith cranked the van around the corner, heading left again.

"Where are you going, Keith?" I could see Keith's eyes flashing back and forth from the road to the rearview mirror.

"Shut up, Rob!" Keith yelled.

There was a bend in the road ahead of us, but even before we'd turned the corner, I could see the giant mound of snow.

"What the hell is that?" Alan shouted.

Keith slammed on the brakes, and the van slid sideways into the mountain of snow. "What the fuck? Who does this?" he yelled, slamming his hands against the steering wheel.

"I thought you knew the way out," Alan said. The pickups had come to a stop, their headlights filling the van with blinding, white beams.

"Goddamn. Why would you dump all the snow in one place?" Keith whined. "Idiots. These people are idiots." Being new to town, I'd noticed giant piles of snow like this in a number of places. There was one right outside our high school, growing larger and dirtier every day.

"Get us out of here, Keith," Alan said.

Keith shook his head.

"They've blocked the road." He locked the doors and rolled up his window. Guys were starting to get out of the trucks. Four, six, eight. More, maybe. I don't think I ever found out how many guys there were.

How many lives were forever changed on that freezing cold night.

Chapter Three

"Open the door." The kid's face was close to the window. I knew him from school, although my first thought was that this was the first time I'd ever heard his voice.

"Guys," Keith said. "It was a joke."

The kid's breath steamed the window. "Open."

"It was just Devon Warren I was after," Keith yelled. "He's been messing with my girl."

What happened next happened so fast that I didn't even fully understand what was going on. The large side window behind Keith exploded. Something came into the van, sending glass flying everywhere. I covered my head. When I looked up again, Keith's door was open, and he was being dragged out of the van.

I pushed back against the passenger-side door.

"What the hell?" Alan said.

One guy had a hold of Keith. He was twisting him around, back and forth, when suddenly Keith's head snapped back. Bright-red blood flew into the air. He was heaved against the side of the van, then thrown to the ground.

One of the boys got in the back of the van and grabbed Alan. It was like he'd been sucked out the door by nothing more than a wind. He went down fast, thrown across the snow and into the crowd.

I undid my seat belt and bolted across the driver's seat and out the door. I thought I could talk to them. Reason with them. Explain that it had been a mistake. That Keith was just angry about losing his girlfriend. Everyone would understand that, right?

I got as far as "Guys" before someone punched me. It was a hard, closed-fist slam to the side of my head, and it sent me reeling. I grabbed onto the side mirror, but my weight broke it off, and I was on the ground before I knew what was happening. Someone kicked me in the stomach. I rolled over, and now all I could see was the rim of the front tire. Someone grabbed me and rolled me onto my back.

"Why'd you come in here?"

I knew this guy. Duncan something. We were in English together. He'd done a project on *The Absolutely True Diary of a Part-Time Indian*, which some of the other kids had made fun of after. But his presentation was really good. He'd talked about the book, the author and how he related to it. Did a way better job of it than the kids who presented "True Love in *Twilight*" or "Fault in *The Fault in Our Stars*." I wanted to tell him this, but I couldn't speak. I spit out a gob of blood.

More people were arriving. Coming out of the nearby houses. Adults, I thought. Someone would put a stop to this. It was a stupid prank. We'd learned our lesson.

Keith was down on the ground. One guy was sitting on him. Another guy walked up and kicked him in the face. His head swung farther around than it should be able to, then back again.

There were dots of blood on the ground. The big moon lit the scene in a cool, natural light.

"Duncan," I managed. "It was—"

He punched me, hard, in the stomach. I couldn't find air again. I sucked at nothing, pulling and pulling, trying to bring oxygen into my lungs. There was an older guy standing beside Duncan, swaying from side to side.

"Hit him again," the guy calmly said. Duncan got on top of me and hit me again. I couldn't feel much though. Just this endless search for air.

There was a scuffle to my left. I managed to get a sliver of air into my lungs as I turned my head. It was Alan. He'd somehow broken free from the grasp of the guy holding him. He was up, moving in a stumbling run back down the road. Keith was unconscious. Out on his back, arms spread. I heard someone suggest they tie his arms and legs to the back of the pickups. Stretch him out a little.

Duncan's weight on me was horrible. He had his elbow planted on the side of my head. The ground was freezing. My ear stung from the cold. I turned my eyes up to see Alan darting around the front of the closest pickup. There were guys waiting for him, so he darted back the other way. He stumbled as he came around the front, but it looked like he had a clear shot up the road.

Run, Alan, I thought. Get out of here.

He made it to the rear of the pickup and then, very suddenly, was thrown back to the ground.

"Ho shit!" someone yelled. There was laughter, but the stuttered kind people produce when they don't know what to do. Alan was down on the ground. He wasn't moving.

"Why'd you guys come in here?" Duncan said to me. "Why'd you have to do that?"

"Hit him again!" the older guy above me said.

"I got this," Duncan said.

"No you don't. Hit him, I said."

Alan wasn't moving. He was a lump on the ground in the glare of the headlights. Two guys bent over him. One prodded him and looked at the other.

"I got this," Duncan repeated. He shifted slightly. I brought my head up off the ground. A moment later all I could see was the toe end of a boot. My head snapped back against the van's tire, and I was out.

Chapter Four

THREE DAYS LATER

"It was one of these guys who hit your friend with a shovel," the detective said. He'd placed a sheet of photos in front of me, and his index finger was locked beside one of the men. Every time he picked up the page of photos, his finger went to the same spot.

"It was dark," I said.

"You saw some faces though."

"Sure. But I can't be certain."

"Try harder."

What did that even mean? *Try harder*? I stared at the photos. I recognized a few of the guys from that night, but I couldn't say if any of them was the one who'd hit Alan.

Alan, who remained in a coma. His brain had been swelling, and the only way to keep it from killing him was to put him in a chemically induced coma and wait.

I had visited him that morning, and it was scary as hell. He was just lying in his bed, his face completely emotionless. Tubes shooting out of him in all directions. Machines beeping and humming.

"I've seen these guys at school," I said. I pointed at two of them. "But I don't know if they were there that night."

"We know. You've told us that. We have spoken to everyone there, and charges are going to be laid. But there's a kid in a coma. He might not make it. One of these guys hit Alan in the head with a shovel." His finger tapped on the photo, and then he sat back in his chair. He was a big, meaty guy with a thick mustache. So cop that if you saw him in shorts and a T-shirt playing volleyball on the beach, you'd think, That dude's a cop.

"I didn't see the guy who hit him, sir," I said.

"You can call me Ben," he said. "Or Detective Darbyshire, if you like."

"Okay."

"Listen, what happened that night is awful. All of it. You guys shouldn't have been there doing what you were doing..." I opened my mouth, and he held a hand up. "I know, I know, you didn't do anything yourself. You didn't throw anything or yell anything. You were stuck in the van. Wrong place, wrong time. Even your buddy Keith admits to that."

"He's not my buddy," I said, talking over him. The detective stopped, closed his lips really tight, then went on. "Nevertheless, you were there, and an awful thing happened. Okay? And when awful things happen, we have to deal with them. The police have to find whoever it is that did these awful things and bring them to justice." He sat forward again and put his finger on the same picture. "One of these guys has been identified as a possible suspect."

"Yeah?" I said.

"More than one person has identified the same individual. But we can't go entirely on their word. You understand? We need someone else to tell us exactly what happened."

“These other guys already said who hit Alan?”

“I can’t get into other people’s testimonies. But without someone being brave and stepping forward, we can’t do anything about it. Do you see what I’m saying?”

I stared at the pictures again. Duncan was there, and so was another kid I knew from school, Marc. It was strange to see their photos in a lineup. It meant they’d been brought into the police station before.

It meant they had done something wrong.

“I saw one older guy there,” I said.

“Okay.”

“But I don’t think he’s in any of these pictures.”

“You’re talking about Gerry Legland. The tall guy with a general lack of follicle coverage on his head.”

"Yeah. He was the one who kicked me in the face," I said.

"Sure, you've told us that. But if he was beside you, then he couldn't have hit your friend with a shovel, could he..."

"I guess not."

"So let's forget about Gerry. There are charges against Gerry right now for his part in this." Detective Darbyshire leaned forward and planted his finger again. Something about it felt like a last chance. "And focus on who it was that had the shovel." I stared at the photos. I went through each of them one by one. I closed my eyes and tried to remember that night. Tried to remember all the faces as they flashed in and out of the headlights. A bank of clouds had shifted, letting the moon cover the area in that silvery light. But when it came right down to it, I couldn't see the face of the guy who'd grabbed Alan. In fact, as far as I could recall, he'd never even turned my way.

"I'm sorry," I said.

I had a teacher back in fourth grade who caught me red-handed stealing pencils out of his desk. When he brought me to the principal's office, I refused to admit to the crime. I denied and denied and denied. I remembered the look on that teacher's face. It was the same one the detective was giving me now. Disappointment. Sadness. A complete lack of understanding. The only difference was that back in fourth grade I'd been lying. This time I was telling the truth.

"Fine," he said, closing the book and standing up. "You don't know, you don't know." He headed for the door. "You'll go before a judge on Wednesday." I knew this already. I thought I'd get off light. I mean, I hadn't really done anything. But I'd been there, and that was enough. I hadn't tried to stop Keith either, which was something I was going to have to live with. "He'll ask me how repentant I think you are about this crime. I'm not sure what I can tell him."

"I didn't do anything," I said for the hundredth time.

He tapped the book as he opened the door. "Your mom's waiting for you in the lobby. See you in two days." And with that he was gone.

Chapter Five

The judge was not kind to us. Keith and I heard a lot about respect. About community. About understanding differences and finding similarities.

About kindness.

Keith nodded to everything, saying, "Yes, Your Honor. Yes." But when the judge looked away, I caught him glaring at Duncan and the kid standing next to him, Marc. When the final decision came down, Keith clenched his fists.

"One hundred hours of community service for all four of you," the judge said. "I want you to listen to me, boys. We live in a community that is tolerant. Whatever perceived differences you feel you might have, they amount to very little in the end. To help you better understand this, I am arranging to have the four of you work together. Maybe you can find some common ground." He waved us away.

As I was walking out of the courtroom, Detective Darbyshire stepped up beside me.

"I can still put in a good word for you," he said. "Get those hours reduced. Get you working somewhere easy."

"I still don't know," I said.

He gave me the strangest look. "I don't get you, kid. You point a finger, and this is all over. Like that."

He snapped his fingers, then walked away, shaking his head.

The next day the four of us were standing outside the old primary school. Keith flicked a cigarette into a snowbank as a crappy minivan pulled up. Someone had the big idea of cleaning the place up and making "something" of it. So far, no one knew what that something would be. A lot of ideas had been floated around. Everything from a dance studio to a gymnastics gym to a skate park. Whatever was finally decided, the place had to be cleaned.

"This is a fucking mess," Keith said.

The social worker assigned to watch over us agreed. His name was Roger—or Rog, as he wanted us to call him. "It's been sitting here for five years with no one to care for it," he said.

Rog was a thin guy with a shock of blond hair sticking straight up off his head. He wore wire-rimmed glasses and had sliced the hell out of his neck shaving that morning. Bits of toilet paper clung to the red grooves. He opened the door and let us into the building.

"Freezing in here," Marc said.

"Yup," Rog said. "I'd suggest you get going. You know, work up a sweat."

"This is bullshit," said Keith. His face was covered in bruises, and I could tell his right arm still hurt. He limped a little as well, though he'd denied it when I'd mentioned it earlier.

"It's your fault," Marc said.

Keith sniffed, ignoring him. He grabbed a broom and walked away from us.

"I'd get some organization if I were you," Rog said. "Make a plan first, or you'll just be pushing dirt at one another all day." Keith and Marc ignored him, moving to opposite sides of the room. "Suit yourselves. This place has been a disaster for years.It can't get much worse."

I followed Keith because it seemed like the right thing to do. I could have hung with Duncan, but he had immediately followed Marc. Duncan was cool. He was smart and funny and said the strangest things in class, things that days later you'd still be thinking about. Marc, on the other hand, always seemed angry at the world. As though it owed him something. Or someone did.

After seeing all the bruises on Keith, I knew Duncan had been protecting me that night. He'd hit me, for sure, but not like Keith had been hit.

Not like Alan had been hit.

"He's right, you know," I said to Keith. "We should have a plan or something, or it'll just become a bigger mess."

"I'm not working with those guys," Keith replied. "They stink." I hadn't noticed anything specific. We were a bunch of teenage boys. We all stank. Keith kept talking. "We can just go this way, and if they're smart they'll do the same on their own end. Eventually we'll meet up."

Keith started sweeping across the floor. I followed, turning my back to Duncan and Marc. We worked for about five minutes before I looked up to see Duncan and Marc doing the same as us. I put my head back down and kept going. All of two minutes later, a little ball of dust flew up around me. I stopped just before ramming into Marc, who had, for some reason, decided to change directions and was suddenly on our side of the room.

"Dude," I said. He kept going, sweeping over what we'd already done and leaving a trail of debris.

"What the hell are you doing?" Keith demanded. Marc didn't reply. He hit the end of the room and turned around. "Hey! I'm talking to you."

I looked over to where Rog should have been. All I saw was an empty chair. I could see him outside the window, smoking a cigarette in the freezing cold. I turned back to see Keith tossing his broom to the floor.

"I'm going to ask you one last time," he said. Marc kept walking, and a second later Keith was taking steps toward him. Marc was fast though. He dropped his broom and turned, deflecting Keith's first punch and coming in low with one of his own. Keith rotated off Marc and slid to a stop. He looked like a wrestler going in for a takedown. His arms were low, his eyes locked on Marc. Marc sniffed, then took a quick step forward and did a little stutter punch. Keith flinched, and Marc laughed.

"Ha," Marc said. "You're afraid of me."

"No I'm not."

"Whatever," Marc said. He let his arms drop. "You're not even worth it."

Keith didn't wait to run at Marc again. This time Marc wasn't fast enough, and Keith caught him on the side of the head with a clean, hard roundhouse. Marc went down, and Keith was immediately on top of him.

"Keith, shit, man, what the hell!" I said. I reached down to try and stop him, but he had Marc's arms pinned and had already landed two quick shots to his head. I grabbed at Keith's arm, and he pushed me aside. I stumbled, falling backward.

"Keith," I said. "Quit it." Keith had his arm raised, his fist cocked, ready for another punch, when he was suddenly tossed to the ground. Duncan stepped over Marc and shoved Keith into the wall with a foot. Keith immediately scrambled to stand.

"Stay down," Duncan warned.

"Fuckin' injuns," Keith replied.

"Call us what you will, but if you ever touch him again there will be hell to pay."

"You sure about that?" Keith said.

"Hey, what the hell?" Rog yelled. "I leave you alone for two minutes and you guys are at each other's throats?" Cold air whipped through the room. Roger closed the door without taking his eyes off us. Duncan continued to stand over Keith as Marc got to his feet. There was blood dripping from Marc's mouth, and he seemed to be swaying slightly.

"You guys stay on your side of the room," Keith said as he pulled himself up against the wall. "And we'll stay on ours." Duncan didn't reply.

He let Keith walk around him. Eventually he turned and returned to the other side of the room.

"I don't get paid enough to deal with this shit," Rog said before he sat back down and flicked open his newspaper. "Not even close."

Chapter Six

Alan died the next morning.

It was the same day a vicious winter storm swept in. The city gave up and stayed home. And in the middle of that quiet chaos, Alan's body quit.

I received a phone call from his brother and spent the rest of the morning unable to move. I hadn't known Alan for long, but the circumstances surrounding his death were difficult to process. The fact that I had been there. That we had done what we had done, whether out of cowardice or hatred or whatever. In the end, a kid had died.

The following day I awoke to find Rog at my door.

"Let's go," he said, stepping inside and slamming the door behind him.

"Where?" I asked.

"Falcon Lake." He removed his wool hat and banged the snow from it. "They're snowed in, and we need to bring supplies up, then shovel out a couple of other community buildings."

"Where's Falcon Lake?" I said.

"About an hour and a half north."

I looked out the window. The snow was still coming down, but much more lightly. A plow had gone by and left a massive snowbank at the end of our driveway. I stood there staring at the van idling on the street and Rog's deep footprints in the snow.

I wanted someone to tell me what to do. To drag me from one place to another, then put my hands and mind to work. Anything to block the vision of Alan flying through the air and then lying motionless on the ground.

"I'm sorry about your friend," Rog said. He seemed ready to go on but then didn't. Instead he replaced his hat and put his hand on my shoulder. "We'll stop for something to eat before we get the other guys."

"What other guys?"

"All four of you are coming," he said, opening the door. "I'll be in the van."

An hour later we were on the road heading north. I would call it a highway, but that would bring up images much grander than the reality. We're talking two lanes here. At times those two lanes weren't wide enough for vehicles to actually pass one another.

Luckily, there weren't many other people stupid enough to be driving that day.

Somehow I'd managed to get shotgun. Duncan and Marc were in the middle seats while Keith had set himself up in the very back. Rog had hooked his phone up to the stereo and was playing some really old rock.

I must have looked like I was grooving a little during a Led Zeppelin tune because Rog suddenly started asking me a million questions. Questions that began with my musical likes and somehow wound around to my brother.

"How many more years does he have?" Rog asked.

"A little over five," I said, keeping my voice low. For some reason, I didn't want Duncan and Marc to hear the discussion.

"Must be hard for you and your mom." Rog kept his eyes on the road. He never looked over at me. The sky was that heavy white you get in winter where the sun manages to filter through and then the snow traps the light and creates a blinding glare.

"She goes to visit," I said.

"You don't?"

"He said he didn't want me to," I said. "He doesn't want me to see him in there or whatever."

"Sometimes people do things thinking they're protecting us when actually what everyone needs is the exact opposite."

I thought about this for a moment. It sounded like a riddle. We hadn't seen another car in at least half an hour.

The road was still snow-covered, as if the plow had gone through really fast and just barely managed to scrape the massive amount of snow aside.

"Do you see what I mean?" Rog began.

But he didn't get to finish. He'd turned to look at me for a second, and as he was turning back to look at the road, the van shifted and smashed into the snowbank. A second later we were spinning. Rog's arm flew out and hit me in the chest just before my head was about to ring off the dashboard. I felt all the air drain from my lungs.

Everyone was yelling as if Rog could suddenly fix the situation. As if he'd made a decision to smash into the snowbank. The van went up on one side, and the next thing I knew we were rolling down an embankment. I was terrified, but at the same time I had a weird sense that nothing bad was going to happen.

I can't explain why this was or even exactly what it felt like. I just believed that I'd be fine and that everyone in the van would be fine. That we'd walk away from this and I'd be back home that afternoon, comfortable and warm, listening to the wind howl outside.

Too bad I was totally wrong.

Chapter Seven

I must have blacked out, because the next thing I remember was staring into the dead white sky through a crack in the windshield. Sounds came at me in swirls until the swirls became voices.

"Is everyone okay?" I said. It sounded like someone else said it. I turned. Duncan was rotating his arm in small circles as if he thought it might be broken and wanted to make sure he still could. Marc was beside him. I guess it was the shock or adrenaline or something, but Marc didn't seem to notice that there was a jagged piece of glass stuck in his shoulder. I started to say something, but then Keith was yelling.

"Get this off my legs!" I could see Keith's arm sticking out from between two boxes of the supplies we'd brought.

"Keith," I said. Or maybe I didn't. I really couldn't tell. The wind was howling through the van. My neck hurt as I tried to move. Everything felt as though it were happening to someone else and I was only a spectator.

I heard Duncan say, "Marc, something is stuck in your arm." I looked over at Rog. His head was turned toward me. His eyes were closed. There was a cut on his forehead. The driver's-side door was crumpled and pushed up against his shoulder, and the steering wheel was tight against his thighs.

I unhooked my seat belt.

"What the hell?" Marc yelled, clueing in. "Get it out, get it out!"

"I don't know if we should," Duncan replied. "It might just make you bleed more."

"Roger," Marc said. "Ask Roger!"

"Roger is out," I said. The wind was smashing pellets of snow into the van, making little tinging sounds.

"What do you mean *out*?" Duncan said. He unhooked his seat belt and leaned forward. He shoved Roger. A little moan escaped Roger's lips, and his eyes fluttered. "Come on, Rog, wake up."

"He's really stuck in there," I said. "I don't think you should shake him like that." The van had basically collapsed around him.

"Is there a first-aid kit or something?" Duncan asked.

"Maybe in the back," I said. Duncan sat down, and I swung between the front seats and toward the back. I lifted one of the boxes off Keith but struggled to get a hold of the next one. The van was tilted skyward and to the driver's side, so the front end was high and the boxes of supplies had come down hard.

"You okay?" I said.

"Just get these off me!" Keith pushed at the boxes. I pulled another one out, then a third, which finally released him. "What the fuck happened? I was asleep."

"We went off the road."

"That's obvious. Why?"

"I guess we hit some ice or something. I don't know."

Keith looked out the window. "Where the hell are we?"

The storm seemed to be getting worse. I couldn't see more than ten feet, and even then everything was just different shades of white.

"I think we went down an embankment," I said.

Marc started freaking out. As I turned back to him, he yanked out the piece of glass. A spurt of blood swept across the window.

"Wrap something around it!" I yelled. Duncan grabbed a towel from between the front seats and quickly wrapped it around Marc's arm. Marc had been gasping for breath, but then, as though a switch had been flicked, he calmed down. "Make sure it's tight," he said.

"Is he going to be all right?" Duncan said, looking at me.

"I don't know," I replied. "I'm not a doctor or anything." Keith moved onto the middle seat. His face was already starting to bruise from where the boxes had struck him.

"You got blood all over the place," Keith said.

"Shut up," Duncan said without looking at him.

"That's disgusting, man."

The wind shook the van. Keith shifted to the end of the middle seat and opened the side door.

"Close the door, moron," Duncan said.

"I'm going to see where the hell we are," Keith replied before jumping outside.

"Really?" I said.

"What, you want us to sit here and freeze to death?" he said. "I'll be right back." He pulled his hat out of a pocket and yanked it low on his head.

"Can you close the door?" Duncan asked. I pulled on the handle, but it wouldn't budge. Keith had already been swallowed up by the storm.

"It's stuck," I said. Duncan moved across the seat until he could grab the handle. We tried pulling together, but the door was jammed.

"What an asshole," Duncan said. "We can't stay in here. We'll freeze."

"Where are we supposed to go?" I said.

"We have to wake up Rog." I left the door and returned to the front seats. Roger hadn't moved. His head remained slumped to one side. His glasses dangled from one ear. I propped his glasses back up and undid his seat belt. His legs looked strange beneath the steering wheel. Like they'd been clamped there.

"Rog. Hey, Rog. You there?" I said. He didn't move. I had no idea how we would get him out of his seat.

"Holy shit," Keith said as he scrambled back into the van. "That's not an embankment. We went over a fucking cliff."

"What? How high?" I said.

"Twenty feet maybe. I don't know. It's storming like hell out there. You can barely see where you're going." Keith started yanking on the door. "Why won't this close?"

"It's jammed," I said.

"We have to get this shut," Keith said. "It's freezing in here."

"It won't move," Duncan said. Because of how loud the wind was, everyone had to shout.

"Maybe you could help?" Keith kept hauling on the door. Duncan reached around him and tried pulling it as well, but it wouldn't move. The inside of the van was turning white from the blowing snow. It must have dropped five or ten degrees already.

"Whoa!"

I turned to find Roger sitting up, shaking his head. "What?" he said. A great sense of relief washed over me. Sure, we were stuck at the bottom of a cliff, freezing to death, but at least now everyone would stop asking me what we should do.

"You okay?" I said. Roger was staring out the front window as though he was still driving.

"What happened?"

"We went off a fucking cliff," Keith said. "And now we're going to freeze to death."

"We're not going to freeze to death," Marc said.

"How so, Tonto?"

"We can get out of here."

Roger shifted. "I'm stuck." He reached down beside him and pulled on the lever there. The seat shifted a little. He cringed and groaned as the chair shifted back and his legs slid out from beneath the steering wheel.

"Are you okay?" I said again. The wind was ramping up. The sound of it was overwhelming.

"I don't know. But Marc is right. We need to get out of here."

"Where the hell are we going?" said Keith.

"Grab what you can from those boxes. There should be a first-aid kit and matches. Some tarps and things. Whatever you can easily carry." Rog swung himself off the seat, grimacing as he moved his legs.

Keith got into the boxes and started handing items over to Marc as I opened the passenger door and tried to help Roger get out.

"I can't put any weight on my left leg," Rog said. "You're going to have to help me."

"Okay," I said. "Where are we going?"

Roger looked around. "We need to get into the forest. It's too open here. There are cabins all along the river. We just need to find one. If not, we can build a shelter and start a fire." I remembered we'd been driving beside a river the whole way up. I'd seen cabins along the shore.

Keith, Duncan and Marc piled out of the van. Then they just stood there looking at us.

"We're going to die," Keith finally said matter-of-factly. He looked at Duncan and said, "When spring comes, someone will dig up three perfectly nice guys and two fuckin' injuns."

Chapter Eight

"Put me down, put me down," Rog said. I helped him lean against a tree, and he slid to the snowy ground. The wind was much calmer in the woods. The treetops above swayed from side to side, but for the most part the giant evergreens insulated us from the worst of the storm.

"We need to get that tarp set up somewhere to block the wind," Rog said, pointing at the cliff face. "There, against the cliff side where the trees are. And we need some dry wood to start a fire."

"I'll help Keith with the tarp," I said.

"No, you go with Marc to get wood. Leave these two here." I didn't like the idea at all. Not because I thought Keith and Duncan were going to start brawling again, but because I didn't want to be alone with Marc. I wasn't afraid of him or anything. I just didn't trust him. I felt like if he saw some way of getting himself out of danger, he'd take it and not much care what happened to the rest of us.

"Come on," Marc said. I followed in his footsteps. We both pulled dead and brittle branches from wherever we could reach.

"We're going to need bigger stuff to actually keep a fire going," I said. "This will burn out in minutes."

"Yeah yeah," Marc said. He didn't seem to be looking at the ground. Instead he was craning his neck to see around the trees. "Do you know what time it is?"

I pulled my phone out. There wasn't a signal, and the battery was getting really low. "Just after three."

"It's going to be dark soon."

I almost tripped over a downed tree. Thick branches stuck straight up along its top. Branches thick enough to burn like logs.

"These could keep us going for a while," I said.

"Get as many as you can," Marc replied. "Then let's head back." I snapped a couple of branches off and laid them on the ground. I was so focused on getting more wood that I didn't notice Marc just standing there staring at me.

"What?" I said when I finally did notice him.

"Why do you guys hate us so much?" he asked.

"What?"

"You heard me."

"I don't hate anyone," I said, then for some reason added, "I just moved here."

"There aren't any Indigenous people where you're from?"

"Sure, yeah, of course there were. I even had a friend who was part native, er…Indigenous."

"That was awfully kind of you."

"I didn't mean it that way. I meant, I don't really care. I don't see people that way. Or, at least, I try not to."

"What way is that?"

"By their heritage, I guess?" I said. I didn't know what I was saying. Of course I saw people's heritage. Of course I knew that my friend Moe was from the Middle East, Jaden was black, and Finn was from Ireland. It was part of them. How they looked. Their culture.

But it wasn't everything.

"Your friend Keith cares."

Marc was right. And none of us would have been here if it hadn't been for him and his redneck anger issues. And Alan wouldn't be dead. But for some reason I found myself defending him.

"I don't think it's anything personal," said.

"Not personal?"

"Like, I mean, he doesn't hate *you*," I said.

"Just *my kind*."

I ripped another branch off the log and gathered up everything I could.

“That might be worse,” Marc said.

“I can’t explain it.”

“I can. He’s an asshole.”

“That definitely is part of it,” I said.

Marc gave me a half smile, then gathered up all he could, and we started back. To save energy, I kept to where we had already made holes in the snow.

“Why did you guys even come to the reserve that night?” Marc asked after a while.

I stopped and put down my bundle of branches. I had to readjust it before trying to move on. But I also needed time to figure out how to describe as clearly as possible what I thought had happened.

“Keith said he did it because Devon Warren had been messing with his ex-girlfriend.”

“Who’s his ex?”

“Michelle Cooper.”

Marc laughed.

"What?" I said.

"That girl was after Devon. The feeling was not mutual." We got moving again. I could hear voices in the distance.

"He didn't go there to get back at Devon. You know that, right?" Marc said quietly.

"That's what he said."

"Sure, that's what he *said*. But the truth is, he went there to prove he was better than us. That he could chuck moldy fruit at us and we couldn't do shit about it."

"I don't know," I said.

"I do," Marc replied. "And I think you do too."

Duncan and Keith had the tarp set up and had somehow dug out an area just in front of it for a fire pit. As soon as Marc spotted Keith, he dropped the wood he was carrying and sat down on a log beside Duncan, on the other side of the fire pit.

"What took you two so long?" Keith said. "We're fucking freezing."

I dumped my bundle of branches in front of him. Everything about him left me feeling bad. Bad for him, though, not for myself. "There's not much out there."

"We're surrounded by wood," Keith said, laughing. He got down and made a little triangle of the smaller pieces, then set a wad of paper in the middle. Before he lit it, he looked up with a grin and said, "It looks like a little teepee, doesn't it?" Moments later the fire had taken hold, and he began stacking more wood around it in the same triangular shape. "Amazing how easily they go up." Luckily, Marc and Duncan were ignoring him.

"Chill out, Keith," I said.

"What? I'm just making an observation."

"Well, quit it." I didn't normally stand up to this kind of stuff. I mean,

I'd heard comments like that all my life, and I'd just let them go. Mostly because when someone says something like this, you're just happy it isn't about you. That you're not on the side people are laughing at. But when people discovered my brother was in jail, I had a taste of what it felt like to be on that side. I became a person some people wanted to stay away from. Like making poor decisions ran in the family.

It didn't take long for the fire to grow big enough to be a heat source. Rog came over to where we were standing with our hands out, feeling the warmth of the flames.

"We're going to have to work together like this to survive," Rog said. "This is no joke out here."

"The road's no more than a mile from here," Keith said. "As soon as this storm clears we'll walk out of here and hitch a ride. Someone has to know we've gone missing by now anyway."

"It's not that easy," Duncan said.

"Sure it is."

"Which way is the road?" Duncan inquired.

Keith looked around for a moment, then pointed.

"Wrong," said Duncan.

"Okay, chief, which way is it?"

Duncan pointed in an entirely different direction.

"And how can you be so sure? Did your *spirit animal* tell you?" asked Keith with a sneer.

"I paid attention when we left," Duncan said. "You have to know nature. Be a part of nature."

"Listen to this bullshit," Keith said. "Are *you* one with nature, Rob?"

"I knew where the road was," I said.

"You have redskin blood in you?"

"You have no respect," Duncan said. He didn't seem mad though. Or offended. He just seemed tired. "We're individuals. People. You don't have to treat us like a group. Take a person as he is."

Keith shook his head and stared at the fire. He didn't seem to have anything to offer in response, which was refreshing.

The storm continued to blow, whipping the trees around above our heads.

"We'll all need to sleep here tonight," Rog said. Evening was already setting in. Soon it would be too dark to go tramping around in the forest. There was a lake nearby, and the last thing we needed was someone falling through the ice. Keith and Duncan had strung the tarp up on a couple of trees. It wasn't so much a tent as it was a bit of a wind barrier. Rog, Duncan, Marc and I started toward the sad-looking enclosure. I was sure it would be the most uncomfortable night of my life.

"I'll stay out here, thanks," Keith said.

And he did. Like a complete maniac, Keith sat beside the fire all night, holding some kind of bizarre, angry watch over our little camp.

Chapter Nine

I awoke frozen. My fingers and toes ached. I could see my breath with every exhale. It was brutal. Breathing in was like inhaling ice water. I wasn't even certain how I'd slept. I should have been glad that Keith had stayed up all night to tend to the fire, but every time I looked at him there, his back to us, all I could think was that this dislike for people he barely knew was eating him up for absolutely no reason.

Keith glanced over at me as I tried to get up.

"We need more wood. I'll be right back," he said. I didn't reply because I wasn't certain my mouth could move. It took a bit for me to get my arms and legs moving. The tarp we'd been sleeping under was frozen except for the area closest to the fire, where there were little waterfalls trickling to the ground.

Duncan sat up next to me and then stood with what seemed to be very little effort.

"Aren't you frozen?" I managed to say through my chattering teeth.

"My grandfather taught me to slow my breathing when I was cold. You slow your body down like a bear going into a cave to hibernate."

"And that somehow keeps your limbs warm?"

"Those you tuck under you," he said, poking at the fire and putting a final log on. "Keep yourself as tight as possible, but with loose muscles. The main things are your heart and your lungs. That's where the blood goes." Duncan spoke like someone much older than sixteen. I'd noticed this the first day in class. He had a steady pace to his words. As though he was considering them before they left his mouth.

I finally managed to sit up, though everything hurt.

"You need to move," said Marc. He rose beside me and walked to the fire. The towel wrapped around his arm was bright red and seemed damp.

"Get the blood flowing," Marc added.

"Is your arm okay?" I asked as I stood.

"It doesn't hurt," Marc said, glancing down at it. "I'll live."

I pulled my cell out. There was a little battery power left, but still no signal. The wind roared around us.

"What should we do?" I asked.

"There are lots of cabins along the river," Rog said. He stood on his right foot, not putting any weight on his left. I got under his arm and helped him over to the fire. "There has to be one nearby. Most will be stocked. So we can go that way, or we can backtrack and try to find a way up onto the road."

"That's a long way up," Duncan said. "And even if one of us did get up there, how would you manage it?"

"Yeah, that's a real problem." Rog looked at the flames. "I'm sorry I got you boys into this."

"It was an accident," I said.

"I should have been driving slower."

Duncan and Marc remained silent, looking down into the flames.

"Where's Keith?" asked Duncan after a while.

"He went for more wood," I replied. Just as I spoke, Keith came around a large tree, a bundle of sticks in his arms. He dropped them at my feet.

"I kept carrying these even though we don't need them now."

"Why's that?"

"There's a cabin just down there. A ten-minute walk." He looked at Rog. "Maybe fifteen with the state of your leg."

"Does it look like anyone's in it?" Rog asked.

"I didn't go knock on the door," Keith replied. He started kicking snow onto the fire.

"What are you doing?" Marc said, giving him a quick shove.

"We need to put it out before we leave. Unless you want to burn down the forest."

"What if we can't get inside?"

Keith sneered at him. "Oh, we'll get inside, one way or another."

The only door to the small cabin was unlocked, to Keith's disappointment. I could tell he really wanted to smash through it. It was warmer inside, though not by much. The walls didn't seem insulated, but they did block the wind. There was a short stack of firewood outside beneath a tarp and a couple of boxes filled with kindling. Duncan got a fire going in a potbellied stove that sat in the center of the room. The cabin was sparsely furnished. Just a couch, two chairs, a table and, behind a thin curtain, a bed. The one internal door led to a simple bathroom with sink and toilet.

"This is pretty basic," Marc said.

"Feel at home then?" Keith asked.

Marc ignored him. "What should we do now?" he asked, looking to Rog, who had laid himself out on the couch as soon as we got inside. I brought my cell out for the millionth time, hoping somehow it would suddenly catch a signal. Still nothing.

"See if there's a two-way radio in here somewhere," said Rog. "This looks like a hunting cabin. Sometimes the hunters keep two-ways for emergencies."

The three of us dug around the cabin but didn't find any radios. We did find some cans of beans and soup though. Marc got out a couple of pots and soon had food bubbling away on top of the woodstove.

"Someone's going to come looking for us, right?" I said. I seemed to be the only one really concerned.

"Certainly, soon enough," said Rog. "The storm has lifted here, but that doesn't mean it hasn't settled in somewhere else. Either back home or farther north. I was supposed to check in once we arrived. But still, we can't count on anyone but ourselves for now." He winced as he shifted slightly.

"Are you okay?"

"Likely fine. Is there any more Tylenol in that first-aid kit?"

I opened the kit and found a single pill in the bottle. How he'd managed to go through however many had been in there already, I had no idea. "One," I said.

Rog winced again. "I'll save it," he said.

"I'm taking the bed," Keith said. "Wake me when we've been rescued."

"How much food is there?" Rog asked as Marc handed him a bowl of soup.

"Three days, I'd say," Marc said. "Four if we stretch it."

"Let's try to stretch it," Rog said. "There's no telling how long we'll be out here."

Chapter Ten

The weather began to clear late in the afternoon. The small cabin was filled with the warmth of the fire. We'd actually been able to take our jackets off and relax for an hour or so.

Keith had gone outside and dumped a bunch of snow in a pot and was now at the stove, boiling water for coffee.

"Why didn't I think of that?" I said.

"Because you're an idiot. Do you want some?"

"Yeah, sure."

"Rog?"

"Sure," Roger said. "What about you guys? Coffee?"

"I'm good," Marc said.

"Same," Duncan said. They were both standing at the window. Since the snow had stopped and the clouds had cleared, we were actually able to see where we were. Outside there was a wide, open plain beside the river. In the distance, the forest rose up to where the road was. Not that we could see that far.

"My uncle used to have a place up here," Duncan said. "I think it was down the river a ways. I never visited though."

"This is all traditional territory," Marc said.

"All the places no one else wants, eh?" Keith said as he handed Rog a cup of coffee and sat down in one of the chairs.

"My uncle once found an old lacrosse stick when he was digging a well," Duncan said, deciding again to ignore Keith.

"Like, one from the seventies?" Keith said.

"If you mean the seventeen hundreds, then sure," Duncan said.

Keith laughed and said, "No one was playing lacrosse that long ago."

Duncan turned and sat in the other chair. "Did you not know that lacrosse was invented by Indigenous peoples?" he said.

"Bullshit."

"Who do you think it was?" Marc asked.

Keith gulped some coffee. "This French guy," he said. "I forget his name.

I can tell you this for sure, though—no redskin invented lacrosse."

"You're talking about William Beers. He started the first lacrosse league. But our people had been playing the sport for hundreds of years before that. For the Haudenosaunee, the Iroquois, it was originally like a ceremony. A way to give thanks to the Creator. Hundreds of men would play, from sunrise to sunset for two or three days straight."

"No fucking way," Keith said. "How do you play lacrosse with hundreds of people? And you'd be destroyed if you tried to do that for a whole day, never mind two or three."

"Duncan's right," Rog said. "They arranged these giant playing fields, up to two or three miles long. Everything else would stop, and the men would play this game for hours."

"There's no way," Keith said.

"You can research it when we get back to civilization," Rog replied. He rose up on the couch and looked out the window. "Now that the weather has cleared, has anyone checked to see if they have some kind of reception?" We all pulled out our phones. I still had nothing, and Duncan and Marc's phones were dead. Keith thought he had a weak signal and started hitting buttons.

"Can you imagine it?" Duncan said. "Hundreds of men out there all day, rushing back and forth. It must have been incredible to see. Imagine being a part of it."

"I am a part of it," Keith said, still hammering on his phone. "Lacrosse is *our* sport. Lacrosse and hockey, *our* national sports."

"You should be thanking our people for inventing the only thing you're good at," said Marc.

I thought Keith was going to get into it right there. Instead, he kept tapping the screen of his phone.

"There you go again," he said. "Talking about 'your people.' Like it's some big deal what these dudes you never met did. We live now, chief. Not a hundred years ago." He set his phone down. "My battery's dead."

"That's what we all are," Duncan said. "We're all the product of those who came before us. You wouldn't be here if your parents hadn't met. They wouldn't be here if their sets of parents hadn't met. It keeps going back, as far as you can imagine. Farther. It's amazing any of us exist at all. And along the way every culture creates its own sense of identity. Its people define who they are and how they interact with the world. And they create."

"So what?" Keith said. "It took, what, ten minutes for us to come and take all that from you."

Duncan stared at Keith. "If that's the way you want to look at it—"

"It's not a way of looking at it," Keith said. "It's just what happened."

"So now who is dragging up his heritage?" Marc said.

"Just telling it like it is," Keith said. He had that smirk on his face that I hated. Like no matter what he said or did, he was right and, worse, "the winner."

Duncan went back to the window. "Should we try getting to the road?"

"It's going to be night soon. Let's wait until tomorrow morning," Rog replied. "We have plenty of food, a roof over our heads. It's warm here. We can't ask for much more."

"I wonder what it was like," Duncan said. "Back then. Out here. When it was just them and the Creator."

I waited for Keith to say something. Instead, I caught him looking out the window.

"It would have been very different," Rog said. "But in many ways, very much the same."

"How do you think they lasted through these winters?" I asked. "I was totally frozen out there last night."

"We adapt to our environments," Rog said. "It's how humans have managed to survive. We adapt, we grow, we evolve, both physically and mentally." He finished his coffee and set the cup on the floor. "It takes time though. To see a problem and change your thinking. To see the way things are and the way they could be. To discover the ways in which each of us can make a difference." He leaned back on the couch again and sighed.

Marc went to the stove. When he opened the door to put another log in, the room filled with a flash of heat. The wood he added snapped and popped, then sizzled. He stayed there for a moment, his hands before the flames.

The light was so dim in the room, and so bright around him, that for a second I thought he was on fire.

Chapter Eleven

When I woke up the next morning, I saw Marc standing by the woodstove again, slowly stirring another pot of soup. Rog was asleep on the couch, and I could hear Keith's heavy snores from behind the curtained area.

Duncan, sitting at the table, turned to me. "What did the cops ask you?"

"About what?"

"About who hit your friend."

I thought back to the photos. The cop's finger tapping.

"I think they have a suspect," I said. "But I never saw what actually happened to Alan, so I couldn't help them."

"What do you mean you *think* they have a suspect?"

"The cop kept pointing at one of the photos, like he was just waiting for me to tell him that was the guy. He said whoever the guy was, other people had already said it was him or something." Duncan seemed to take this in. Marc poured the soup into three bowls.

"What did the guy look like?" Marc asked.

"He seemed young, maybe in his twenties? He had long hair at the back but short at the top." Duncan and Marc looked at each other.

"The cop seemed desperate for you to say this guy was the one who'd hit your friend?" Duncan asked.

"Yeah," I said. "Very."

Duncan inhaled and said, "That's my brother. But it wasn't him."

"So why are the cops so certain it was?"

"They've been after him for years. I don't know why. He was there that night. But he wouldn't hit anyone with a shovel. Ever."

"So who was it?"

Marc stared into his soup. "It might have been my uncle," he said finally. "It was his shovel. He was there. And he's been real quiet since it happened."

"He'd also been drinking a lot that night," Duncan added. "Which is never a good situation."

"You have to turn him in," I said. "Especially if they think it's Duncan's brother."

"It's not that easy," Marc said. He looked at me intently. "Say someone asked *you* to turn your brother in for what he did. Would you do it?"

I thought about it. Thought about how much I missed Adam. How many days we could have had together doing what brothers do. How much younger my mom might have looked without the weight of his incarceration on her.

But, on the other hand, he was guilty. Because of something he'd done, a girl had died. There was no taking that back.

"I don't know," I admitted.

Marc shrugged. "I don't know either. We can't even be sure it was him."

"What happens if the police arrest your brother?" I asked Duncan. "Won't it seem suspicious if you suddenly give them a different option?"

"They don't have any proof."

"They're pushing your brother as the main suspect," I said. "They'll find someone to point the finger, right?"

"My uncle would stand up then," Marc said. "At least, I hope he would." Marc took our empty bowls and set them on the counter. We hadn't been able to get the water running, but we hadn't tried that hard, to be honest. I think all of us were expecting to be rescued soon enough that there wasn't any need to ration supplies or worry too much about running water.

Not yet anyway.

"You need to tell the truth," Rog said. None of us had noticed he had woken up.

"You heard all that?" Duncan said.

"Absolutely. Did any of you actually see Marc's uncle hit Alan?"

"No," Duncan said. "Everything moved really fast. It could have been him, or it could have been someone else. There's no real way of knowing."

I noticed Marc stayed silent, shifting dishes from one place to another.

"Have you talked to him?" Rog asked, trying to sit up. I could see he was in a lot of pain. Every movement seemed to stab at him.

"He's not the kind of guy you just chat with," Marc said. "Especially if you're going to suggest he killed someone."

"I can help if you like."

"We don't need an outsider in on this," Marc said.

"The offer is there," Rog said. "Rob, could you get me that last Tylenol?" I dug through the first-aid kit and handed him the final pill. He took it without water, then sat back with his eyes closed.

"I am sorry about your friend," Duncan said to me.

"Like fuck you are." The curtain moved, and Keith stepped out into the main space. He'd just taken the bed the night before without asking. My back ached from sleeping in a chair, and I have to say I was pretty pissed at him.

"I wasn't talking to you," Duncan said.

"One of your kind murdered him," Keith said.

"Something that never would have happened if you hadn't come onto the reserve looking to start shit," Marc replied.

"I'm to blame because someone took a shovel to my friend's head?" Keith said. He was still standing just in front of the curtain.

"It never would have happened if you'd stayed where you belonged," Marc said.

"Boys," Rog said, sitting up. "*Enough*."

"I don't have to take this bullshit," Keith said.

"Then leave," Rog said. "Because I can't take your arguing. It was peaceful in here a moment ago. The day is clear. If you can't be civil, go out to the road and get us help."

Keith had been standing right behind Rog, but suddenly he was holding the knife Marc had left on the table and stepping toward Duncan. "My friend is dead, and it's your fault," he said.

Duncan stood up tall, knocking the chair over and backing away.

"Keith," I said. "Relax."

"One of them is going to pay. Or both." He took another step forward. Another step and he was past the couch. Duncan had his hands in front of him, ready. I could see Marc tensing on his back foot.

"Keith!" I yelled.

"Shut up, Rob."

I stepped in front of him. "Put the knife down," I said.

"Someone has to pay for Al," Keith said.

"Alan would still be here if you hadn't decided to drive in there that night," I said. "They're right. You started this."

"I didn't kill Al," he said. His face was red, and his eyes were huge. "*They* did."

"They had nothing to do with it," I said. "We don't know who did. Put the knife down."

Keith took another step forward. "What are you doing, Rob? Defending these savages?"

The word hit something inside me. It made me squirm.

"See, you think the same thing," Keith said. "Somebody has to pay."

"Not like this," I said.

"Exactly like this." Keith took another step, but suddenly, almost too fast for me to even see it, Rog got up off the couch, grabbed Keith's arm and twisted it behind his back until the knife dropped to the floor. Then he threw Keith down.

"This is not happening in here!" Rog yelled, picking up the knife and slamming it onto the table before easing himself back onto the couch. He seemed to be finding it difficult to breathe. Keith stood without a word, opened the door and stomped out.

I ran to the door as he slammed it shut. I opened it again.

"Keith, get back in here," I said. "It's freezing out there."

"No way. I'm done with this. We're a couple of kilometers from the road. I'm heading home."

I turned and said, "Rog, he's going to walk out."

"Let him," Roger said. "We all have to learn when to make choices for ourselves." He closed his eyes. "That's the very base of humanity, Rob. Being able to choose. Once that is gone, so is life." I turned and watched Keith making his way up the slight hill outside the cabin.

"Close the door, man," Marc said. "It's goddamn freezing out there."

Chapter Twelve

We heard the snowmobiles well before we could see them. It was early evening, but already it was pitch dark. Keith had been gone for hours, and even though I was pissed at him, I was also a little worried. But there he was, on the back of the third snowmobile, waving as if he'd single-handedly saved our lives.

The men were part of a search party from Falcon Lake. When we hadn't arrived, they'd started looking for us. Five snowmobiles in all.

We ate together while they explained how they'd found our van and, not long after, Keith. They had two-way radios, so once we'd cleaned up the cabin and put out the fire, they drove us to the road, where a van was waiting to take us home.

Keith seemed to be fishing for praise as our savior. We heard a lot about his frozen fingers and how his boots had filled with snow that turned to icy water. How he'd stood on the side of the road for hours, waiting for a car to pass. How without him, we'd likely all be dead.

Duncan and Marc let it go, never saying a word in response. Eventually, just to shut him up, I said, "Thanks, Keith." And left it at that.

It was three days later before I heard from Rog again. On top of his injuries, he'd managed to get an infection that was causing him no end of issues. He was laid up in hospital, without any idea when he'd be let out. I went to visit. He looked weaker and more frail than he had before.

"I'll get through. It's about making sure I have the right drugs, that's all. I'll heal," he said.

"Are you sure?" I asked. He really looked horrible.

"The body is weak, but the mind is strong," he said with a smile. "What about you? How are you doing?" I thought about it for a while. If I'd gained nothing else from that time in the cabin, it was a better understanding of the importance of choosing my words carefully. Not because I was afraid to offend anyone, but because far too often what we say and what we mean are two completely different things.

Like, I figured Keith using all those racial slurs against Marc and Duncan was actually him saying something about himself. Or his family. Almost as if he was digging at a scar he didn't even know was there.

"I'll be fine," I said.

"What about Marc and Duncan? Have they talked to the police?"

"I don't know," I said. "It wouldn't be easy."

"No," Rog said. "But few things that actually matter ever are." He reached out to pat me on the shoulder. "Take care of yourself. You're a good kid."

No one had ever said that to me, as far as I could remember. At school I sat at the back of the classroom, trying to bring as little attention to myself as possible. My mom was always busy, and even though I knew she thought I was a good kid, or at least that I had been before all that stuff with my brother, she never said it. And my dad...well, he'd left us years before. So long ago that I didn't even really remember him. My brother had become kind of a fill-in. At least for a while. Now he was gone too. So I don't know if it was what Rog said, the way he said it or all I'd just been through, but it was really hard for me to respond. When I did, it was in little more than a whisper.

"Thanks."

The next day I opened the door to find Marc standing on my porch.

"Can I come in?" he asked.

"Yeah, sure." I felt a little odd having him in my house. Not because he was First Nations or anything like that, but because my place was a disaster. And I'd spent the whole morning playing *Grand Theft Auto V* and was a little fuzzy about what reality was.

He sat down on the couch.

"You heard from the cops again?" he asked.

"Yeah." I explained how they had called the day before, asking, after all that had happened, if I might have further information I'd like to share about the attack.

"I talked to my uncle," he said. "I've known him a long time. My whole life. He said it wasn't him."

"Okay," I said.

"The thing is, I know he was lying."

"How?"

Marc looked straight at me. "I saw him do it. I saw him come out of the house. I saw how angry he was. I saw him swing that fucking shovel, and I did nothing." He paused. "But I have to do something now."

"You knew all along?" I said.

"I thought it might go away," he said. "Not the facts, but the feelings.

I thought I could just push through them. Like, you guys came onto the reserve so you deserved whatever happened. But that's not the truth. No one deserved to die that night."

"Alan was a good guy. He didn't want to be there. I didn't either." Which just left Keith, and we both knew it.

"I know," Marc said. "Well, I know that now. But this is going to be hard, man. Did you ever have to testify against your brother?"

"Once—not really testifying though. The cops kept asking me the same questions until I gave them something."

"How'd it feel?"

"Awful. He was already going down, but still."

"Why do you think they did it?"

"The cops?"

"Yeah. Why'd they push you to say anything?"

I thought about this for a moment.

"I guess so I'd have to confront it," I admitted. "So that I had to admit that I knew the kind of person my brother was. The thing is, what he did, selling drugs or whatever, being the middle man, that was the smallest piece of him. He's a great guy. Kind and helpful. And that was what got him in trouble."

Marc kept looking at me. Nodding his head.

"But that little piece of him is now everything, isn't it?" he said. "From here on out, he's an ex-con. A guy who spent time in prison. You don't ever get rid of that."

"Your uncle will be someone who killed a guy," I said flatly.

"Exactly. Our family will be different. People are going to look at us differently. Behave differently. My mother—" he started, then stopped. "He's her older brother. So..."

"Yeah," I said. "It all sucks."

"It fucking blows." He stood up. "But that's what he is. He's a guy who killed a kid with a shovel. No matter what he was before, that's who he is now."

I sat down in the leather chair I always pulled up in front of the TV when I was gaming. This conversation was bringing back too much for me. Not just the night that we drove onto the reserve, but the days before my brother went to jail.

"Listen," Marc said. "This is going to sound weird, but would you come in with me?"

"To the police station?"

"Yeah."

"Sure," I said. For some reason, I hadn't even needed to think about it. "Yeah, sure. Let me get some real clothes on."

At the police station, we asked for Detective Darbyshire and were told to take a seat. It took the detective about ten minutes to get to the station from wherever he'd been. He quickly ushered us into an interview room. He got Marc to sit in the chair normally reserved for suspects while I took one in a corner. As soon as the detective sat down, I moved my chair to the table, sitting right beside Marc.

"So, what's this about?" Detective Darbyshire asked. His eyes were wide and bright, and he almost seemed to be jumping a little in his seat.

"I know who killed that boy," Marc said.

"You are speaking about Alan Callaghan?"

"Yes."

The detective moved his mouth around then sucked his teeth. "You're certain the name you're about to give me is 100 percent correct?"

"Yes," Marc said. "I saw it happen."

"All right, let's hear it."

Marc inhaled. Exhaled. Closed his eyes.

"Tom Nez."

Detective Darbyshire released a long, heavy sigh.

"You sure?"

"Like I said," Marc replied, "I saw it happen. Tom came out of his house, got the shovel from his porch, walked around the front of that van and hit that kid. I don't know if he was going for him or anything. It might have been like an immediate reaction thing."

"You're telling me he wasn't sitting up there in his house and just decided to go down and kill someone."

"I wasn't in his head," Marc said. Then he pushed the chair back as though he was about to leave.

"Sit down, sit down. We'll need this all in writing," Detective Darbyshire said. Then he looked at me. "You have something to add to this?"

"No."

"Why you here then?"

I looked over at Marc. "Just supporting a friend," I said. I got an eyebrow raise for that one.

"A friend. Okay. All right. A friend." Detective Darbyshire plunked a pad of paper and a pen in front of Marc. "You can help him with his spelling."

"I'm sure he'll do fine," I said. Detective Darbyshire got up and left, and for almost half an hour the only sound in the small room was the pen scraping across the paper.

Eventually Marc signed the statement and pushed it away. He looked at me for the first time since the detective had left the room.

"I could tear that up," he said, staring at the paper. "I could make this all stop right here." He kept looking at the paper. Finally he pushed his seat back and stood up. "All right. Let's get the hell out of here." He hammered on the door, and Detective Darbyshire came back in.

"Finished?" the detective asked.

"Finished."

"You sure?"

Marc looked him in the eye and after a beat said, "Yeah, I'm sure." Then we pushed past the detective and through the station.

It was bleak and cold outside. Middle of the afternoon, and already it was getting dark. Marc stopped beside his pickup.

"You need a ride home?" he asked.

"No," I replied. "I'm good."

"Thanks for coming," he said. I nodded to him as he got in his truck and pulled out onto the street. Then he was gone, and I was left standing there. I walked all the way home, feeling entirely different again. When these kind of things happen to you, your world kind of shifts. Like, you expect everything to be a certain way. You wake up in the morning and you're the same guy. You kind of expect each day to go along like the rest of them. But then it doesn't, and you have no option but to start everything over again.

Chapter Thirteen

My brother must have assumed it was my mother waiting for him in the group meeting room because he looked really surprised when he spotted me.

Then angry.

But he came and sat down.

"You look older," he said.

"That's because I am," I replied.

"Mom's showed me pictures and shit." He looked chiseled and tight. Something dark on his skin crept out from beneath his shirt sleeve. There was a look in his eye that hadn't been there before. He seemed...hard.

It was awful.

"You doing okay?" I asked.

He pushed his chair back. "See, this is why I never wanted you to come here." He shook his head at me. "Look where I am. How okay do you think I am? How close to normal is this? Shit, Rob, why'd you come here?"

"To see you," I said. "To talk to my brother again. And to tell you I forgive you."

He seemed on the verge of saying something. But instead he leaned back in his chair and crossed his arms. He looked around the room, then back at me.

"Okay," he said.

"I don't know if that matters or not. And I'm not saying I think anything you did was right. What happened, happened, and it was awful. But no one ever expects something like that will...I mean, after the trial and everything, the school went nuts. Everyone quit partying. I'm sure they started up again soon enough, but for a while there everyone was just trying to be good. Trying to be safe."

"Why are you telling me this?"

"Because you were just a part of it. That's all. You were the guy who sold the drugs that killed a girl, and that's someone you'll always be. But at the same time you're still the person you were before."

"No, I'm not," Adam said.

"I think you are. My brother is still in there." Adam looked at me, and I thought of all the fun we'd had growing up. Playing basketball, listening to music.

Playing vids and watching movies. How we'd been a family. And how all that had changed in one night.

But so much could stay the same as well. It had to. Change can be incredibly fast, but most of the time it's agonizingly slow.

"I want to keep coming to see you," I said.

My brother cleared his throat and wiped at his eyes. "Not a good idea," he said.

"It's not about you, Adam. It's about me. I need my brother," I said. "Even if it's just like this. An hour a week or whatever. I need to see you." In truth, I felt like he needed me as well. To remember who he was.

"All right," he said. "But don't ask me what it's like in here or what's going on and shit. I don't want you to know."

"Okay."

"And don't remind me of how many days I have left in here either. I don't need that shit. It's one day at a time. You get up, get through the day and put it behind you."

"Okay. Fair enough."

"Then, yeah, okay. I think I'd like it if you'd visit." He half smiled at me. "You doing okay?"

"I'm working at it," I said.

We talked for the full hour that day, and I made plans to return the next week. When we said our goodbyes I wanted to hug him so bad, but that wasn't allowed.

Keith was alone when I got to his place. He led me into his kitchen and sat down at an island where he'd been eating cereal.

"Froot Loops?" he said.

"Nah, I'm good."

"That cop call you?" he asked.

"What cop?"

"Darbyshire. About Marc going in and ratting out his uncle."

"No," I said. "What did you tell him?"

"Same thing as before. I didn't see shit." He jammed a big spoonful of cereal into his mouth.

"We never should have been there," I said.

Keith shrugged and kept eating.

"Why do you hate them so much?"

"The injuns?" he said.

"Yeah."

"They think everything should just be handed to them. They don't pay taxes like the rest of us. They live off social assistance and sit around doing sweet dick all. They're a disease on our country."

I stared at him as he spoke. His voice didn't sound right. He sounded like he was repeating a vague rumor he'd heard.

"*A disease on our country*?" I said.

"Listen, the ones that pay into the system, I'm fine with that. But that's not many of them."

"Where are you getting this from?" He was about to answer, but I stopped him. "Better question. What do you have against Marc and Duncan?"

"They're part of the group."

"First Nations," I said.

"Yeah. *First Nations*," he said with his trademark sneer.

"Okay, here's a question. What if they weren't? Then what?"

"What are you asking me?" Keith said. "What I'd think of those two if they weren't injuns?"

"They're just two guys. Marc and Duncan. That's it."

"White guys?" he said.

"Two guys," I said.

He ate another spoonful of cereal, then pushed the bowl away. "That's not how it works," he said. "You can't just take it out. It's all a part of them."

"Exactly," I said. He didn't quite get it, I don't think. I said I had things to do and left without going into it again.

Out on the street, the day had become colder. I pulled my collar up around my ears and bent into the wind. I couldn't help but think of Duncan and Marc. Of Marc's uncle and Duncan's brother. Of my own brother. Of all these people who carried around the weight of their decisions. Carried the weight of what others thought of them, right or wrong. Somewhere in all of this I'd discovered that you can become what people think you are if you let yourself go. But if you stay strong, if you can remember who you were when you were a little kid, what it was you liked to do, the things you said, your feelings...If you are able to remember all these things, then you might change, but you'll always be the same.

I wanted to believe this more than anything. I wanted to believe that the things we do, the choices we make, the words we speak, are only a part of who we are. But I couldn't fully believe it.

That's the part that was hard to take. It was horrible to think of Alan dying on the cold ground that night. I knew he was going to haunt my dreams for years to come. But I didn't feel I was to blame at all. There was nothing I could have done differently. That weight rested on Keith. But then, not entirely. Listening to him, I sensed that he maybe didn't believe everything he was saying. That it had been put there inside him and he didn't know what else to do with it but repeat it over and over.

I understood Marc and Duncan more. In fact, in the weeks to come I hung out with both of them a bunch of times. We'd been through this together, and we'd come out the other side different people.

Jeff Ross is an award-winning author of several novels for young adults, including the Orca Soundings titles *Coming Clean* and *A Dark Truth*. He currently teaches scriptwriting and English at Algonquin College in Ottawa, Ontario, where he lives with his wife and two sons. For more information, visit www.jeffrossbooks.com.

Titles in the Series

orca soundings

Another Miserable Love Song
Brooke Carter

B Negative
Vicki Grant

Back
Norah McClintock

Bang
Norah McClintock

Battle of the Bands
K.L. Denman

Big Guy
Robin Stevenson

Bike Thief
Rita Feutl

Blue Moon
Marilyn Halvorson

Breaking Point
Lesley Choyce

Breathing Fire
Sarah Yi-Mei Tsiang

Breathless
Pam Withers

Bull Rider
Marilyn Halvorson

Bull's Eye
Sarah N. Harvey

Cellular
Ellen Schwartz

Charmed
Carrie Mac

Chill
Colin Frizzell

Comeback
Vicki Grant

Coming Clean
Jeff Ross

Crash
Lesley Choyce

Crush
Carrie Mac

Cuts Like a Knife
Darlene Ryan

Damage
Robin Stevenson

A Dark Truth
Jeff Ross

The Darwin Expedition
Diane Tullson

Dead-End Job
Vicki Grant

Deadly
Sarah N. Harvey

Dead Run
Sean Rodman

Death Wind
William Bell

Desert Slam
Steven Barwin

Down
Norah McClintock

Enough
Mary Jennifer Payne

Exit Point
Laura Langston

Exposure
Patricia Murdoch

Fallout
Nikki Tate

Fastback Beach
Shirlee Smith Matheson

Final Crossing
Sean Rodman

First Time
Meg Tilly

Foolproof
Diane Tullson

Grind
Eric Walters

Hannah's Touch
Laura Langston

The Hemingway Tradition
Kristin Butcher

Hit Squad
James Heneghan

Homecoming
Diane Dakers

Home Invasion
Monique Polak

House Party
Eric Walters

I.D.
Vicki Grant

Identify
Lesley Choyce

Impact
James C. Dekker

Infiltration
Sean Rodman

In Plain Sight
Laura Langston

In the Woods
Robin Stevenson

Jacked
Carrie Mac

Juice
Eric Walters

Kicked Out
Beth Goobie

Knifepoint
Alex Van Tol

Last Ride
Laura Langston

Learning to Fly
Paul Yee

Lockdown
Diane Tullson

Shallow Grave
Alex Van Tol

Shattered
Sarah N. Harvey

Skylark
Sara Cassidy

Sleight of Hand
Natasha Deen

Snitch
Norah McClintock

Something Girl
Beth Goobie

Spiral
K.L. Denman

Sticks and Stones
Beth Goobie

Stuffed
Eric Walters

Tagged
Eric Walters

Tap Out
Sean Rodman

Tell
Norah McClintock

The Way Back
Carrie Mac

Thunderbowl
Lesley Choyce

Tough Trails
Irene Morck

Triggered
Vicki Grant

The Trouble with Liberty
Kristin Butcher

Truth
Tanya Lloyd Kyi

Under Threat
Robin Stevenson

Viral
Alex Van Tol

Wave Warrior
Lesley Choyce

The Way Back
Carrie Mac

Who Owns Kelly Paddik?
Beth Goobie

Yellow Line
Sylvia Olsen

Zee's Way
Kristin Butcher